The Author

Stephanie Dagg lives in Innishannon, County Cork.

She is a mother of two children, Benjamin and Caitlín, and has been writing stories ever since she was a child. Originally from Suffolk in England, she moved to Cork in 1992.

Mentor Press are delighted to be publishing the first three children's titles from this exciting new author: *Oh Mum!*, *The Witch's Dog* and *Escape the Volcano!*

Contents

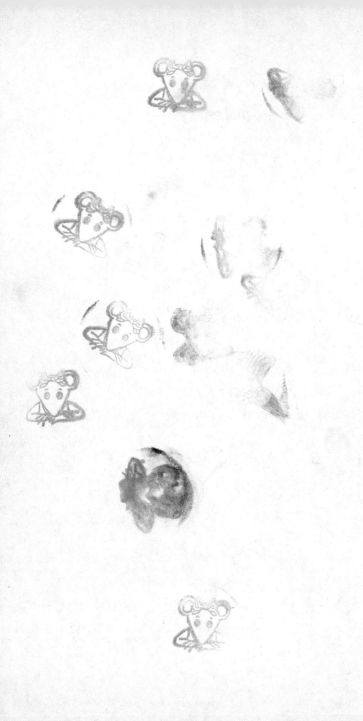

1 A Suitable Pet

Cackling Carol was lonely. After all, she had been living on her own in a cavern for about four hundred years now. There had been plenty of bats, toads, spiders, frogs and nasty creepy-crawlies about in that time, but they didn't count as proper company. Cackling Carol needed a pet.

Most witches have cats, as we all know. The trouble was that Cackling Carol didn't like cats. In fact she loathed them. She hated it when her witchy friends asked her round for a cup of toadstool tea, or a spell-swap session, and she had to stroke their cats and be nice to them. All the time she was thinking how much she would like to put the cats in her cauldron!

So what was Cackling Carol to do? She really wanted a pet – but not a cat. She decided she must find out if there were any other sorts of animal she could have. She went over to her huge, creaky bookcase. She browsed for a moment and then pulled down a big, dusty book from the top shelf, brushed the cobwebs off the cover, and opened it. She turned a few pages until she came across a section on animals.

'Let's see,' she said to herself as she read down the page. Ideally she was looking for an animal that hated cats as much as she did. 'Aardvarks . . . antelopes . . . no, no good . . . cougars . . . dinosaurs – oh, they're extinct, shame . . . dogs. Ahh, dogs!'

Cackling Carol's book told her that dogs were loyal and affectionate but – best of all – liked to chase cats!

The Witch's Dog

'Hee, hee, hee!' cackled Cackling Carol delightedly. 'A dog it shall be then. Come on, Broom. Off we go to find a dog.' Then a thought struck her. 'I wonder . . . where can I get a dog?'

Her broom jumped up from where he was snoozing in a chair and floated gracefully over to Cackling Carol.

'May I may make a suggestion or two?' he asked.

'Oh yes please, Broom,' said Cackling Carol. Her broom was very clever.

'Firstly, the best place to get a dog is from a place called a dogs' home where all the unwanted pet dogs are taken. I'm sure you'd find a suitable dog there. And secondly, you can't go by broom. You'll be very noticeable. It isn't Hallowe'en yet.'

'Good thinking,' said Cackling Carol. 'I'd better turn you into a bicycle then. But first I must take off this cloak and put on my non-witchy outfit. Back in three flicks of lizard's tongue.'

2 The Dogs' Home

Soon they were ready to go. Cackling Carol muttered a few very strange sounding words and Broom at once became a smart red racing bike with drop handlebars and eighteen gears. ('Well, why not be flashy?' thought Cackling Carol.) She pedalled off in the direction of the nearest town. Quite by chance, Cackling Carol came across the dogs' home straight away. She leant her bike up against the wall. She quickly conjured up a bicycle lock for it when she noticed two lads eyeing her bike enviously.

'I wouldn't let anyone steal me,' protested Broom. 'I'd fight them off!'

'Yes, I know, and it would cause a scene. Bikes don't usually start whacking people who try to steal them,' Cackling Carol reminded him. 'Now do try and act the part.'

Cackling Carol trotted through the gate and into a huge yard, surrounded on all sides by kennels. The dogs were yipping, yapping, growling, snapping, whining and woofing – the noise was incredible.

'Frogs' eyeballs!' thought Cackling Carol. 'I didn't know dogs were this noisy.' She began to wonder if perhaps she had opted for the wrong kind of pet.

'Hello!' boomed a hearty voice next to her, making her jump. It was the manager of the dog's home. 'Can I help? What type of dog are you looking for?'

For an instant, Cackling Carol was stumped for words. She hadn't realised there were different types of dogs. She thought they were more or less the same, like cats, only different colours perhaps.

'Oh, I, um . . .,' gabbled Cackling Carol. Then she collected herself. Since her dog would be riding on her broomstick with her then she'd better go for a small one. Broom would moan if the dog was too heavy. (Honestly, he moaned about Cackling Carol sometimes, saying she ate too much pumpkin pie every Hallowe'en.)

'A nice, small dog, please,' she said to the manager.

'This way then,' he said, going towards a far corner. 'All our terriers are over here.'

Cackling Carol started to look in the kennels. The little dogs were very appealing. Carol liked them at once. But despite her normal appearance, the little dogs seemed to sense that Cackling Carol wasn't quite ordinary. As she passed close to them, they snarled and backed into the corner of their kennels, hackles bristling. Cackling Carol was quite upset by it.

'Oh dear,' said the manager, rather surprised. He'd never met anyone who had such a strange effect on dogs before. 'Would you like to look at some slightly larger dogs? Perhaps they'll be more friendly.'

He ushered Cackling Carol to another corner of the yard. But these dogs reacted in the same way. Some even barked angrily at her. Cackling Carol was getting a bit panicky – would someone realise she was a witch? She was just about to dash back to Broom, when she caught sight of the scruffiest, scraggiest – and hugest – dog in the yard. He was in a kennel in the furthest corner of the yard, and he was looking adoringly at Cackling Carol. Cautiously Cackling Carol took a step towards him. The dog wagged his tail. Cackling Carol took another step. The dog wagged his tail even harder.

Taking her courage into her hands, Cackling Carol went right up to the kennel. The dog jumped up in delight and tried to lick her hand through the wire.

Cackling Carol was thrilled.

'This one!' she called to the manager. 'This is the one I want!'

3 Big Roddy

'What! Big Roddy?' gasped the manager. 'But he's enormous. I thought you wanted a small dog?' He looked worried. 'I'm not sure you'll be able to handle him. He's very bouncy.'

'Oh, don't worry. I've got ten strapping great sons at home who'll take him for walks,' fibbed Cackling Carol.

The manager looked relieved. Big Roddy had been at the dogs' home for ages and ages. The manager had begun to think that he would never find a home for him. And he ate so much too (Big Roddy, not the manager!). It would be a very good thing if Big Roddy went today.

'Great!' beamed the manager at Cackling Carol. 'Just come to the office and we'll give you Big Roddy's collar and lead and vaccination record. We need to take your details too. This way.'

He bustled off and Cackling Carol followed him, looking over her shoulder at Big Roddy every few steps. He didn't take his eyes off her for an instant.

At last Cackling Carol and Big Roddy left the dogs' home and found Broom still disguised as a bike.

'Say hello to Big Roddy, Broom,' said Cackling Carol.

Broom said nothing. He was too shocked at the sight of the huge animal! Then he remembered his manners – he really was a very polite broom.

'Delighted to meet you, Big Roddy,' he said weakly. 'I hope you are not as heavy as you look.'

Big Roddy wagged his tail and slobbered affectionately over him.

Cackling Carol wheeled Broom into a quiet side street and, when no one was looking, turned him into a motorbike with a sidecar.

'That's better!' she cackled. She put on her own helmet and then fitted one on Big Roddy's head. He leapt happily into the sidecar and off they went, getting lots of amused looks from passers-by.

Back at the cavern, Cackling Carol changed back into her usual outfit and Broom changed back into a broom. Big Roddy took all these unusual incidents in his stride. He bounced around his new home joyously, sniffing every corner of it and chasing spiders across the floor.

Cackling Carol fussed around happily. She found a spell for making dog food out of leaves and made a whole cauldronful. Then she rummaged through some piles of junk by the back wall and found an old bedspread and cushion for Big Roddy to sleep on.

She came across two old saucepans and, with a bit of magic, turned them into shiny new bowls for Big Roddy – one for his water and the other for his food.

Broom sulked for a little while. He was jealous of all the attention Big Roddy was getting and he was cross at Cackling Carol for getting such a big dog. But when he saw how happy Big Roddy was to have a proper home at last, and how anxious he was to please Cackling Carol, he forgot to be huffy. It wasn't long before he was playing 'Fetch' with Big Roddy. Broom would zoom off for a short distance and Big Roddy would hurtle after him, grab him and carry him carefully back to the cavern. They played for hours.

4 Worrying News

Cackling Carol was just getting supper ready when a big black raven flapped slowly into the cavern with something in its beak. Big Roddy, who had been snoozing, sat up at once and glared at the raven.

'It's OK,' cackled Cackling Carol, stroking Big Roddy's head. 'It's just a messenger raven from Witch Matilda, head of my coven. Let's see what she wants.'

Cackling Carol took the message from the raven. It had been written on a dried frog skin. That usually meant something urgent.

The message read:

Attention Sister Witches

\- - - - - - - - - - - - - - - - - - - -

I have just heard that
Wizard Egbert is in the area.
Be on your guard. Emergency
meeting tomorrow night to
discuss action.

'Bat's toenails!' exclaimed Cackling Carol. 'Wizard Egbert, eh? He's a nasty character. I wonder what he's planning this time.'

Wizard Egbert certainly was nasty. He turned up around Hallowe'en every hundred years or so and caused a lot of trouble. He was a very powerful wizard.

One Hallowe'en he turned all the witches' broomsticks into daffodils just as they were about to set off for a night's witching fun. Then another time he had conjured up an epidemic of frog measles. This made the frogs so poorly that they couldn't be used for spells for months. That had made life miserable for the witches.

'Well, Big Roddy, you'll have to help me watch out for him,' said Cackling Carol, giving a dead rat to the raven for its supper. The raven gobbled it up gratefully. Cackling Carol handed the message back and the raven flapped off to the next witch.

Next day, Cackling Carol was very busy. Since she would be showing Big Roddy off to all her cronies at the meeting, she wanted him to look his best. So she brushed him and combed him and brushed him again, but he still looked a bit scraggy. Even a haircut didn't improve things much.

After dinner, she and Broom gave Big Roddy a lesson in riding on a broomstick. Big Roddy was hopeless. He couldn't stay on for more than a few seconds. He was just too big. So Cackling Carol resorted to shrinking him a bit – well, quite a lot actually – to make him fit on the bristles of the broom. After a few tumbles, Big Roddy got the hang of it, but Broom had to fly very slowly and smoothly.

Soon it was time to go. Cackling Carol hoped Big Roddy would chase the other witches' cats when they got to the meeting. It would make her very unpopular but it would be worth it! Smiling at the thought, she gathered together a few spell books and bottles that might come in useful. She shrank Big Roddy to a suitable size again and off they went.

5 Witch Matilda

Witch Matilda lived a long way away. Broom flew so slowly that Cackling Carol was last to arrive, but at least Big Roddy didn't fall off. The meeting was already underway to judge by the babbling of voices in Matilda's cavern. Cackling Carol quickly got Big Roddy back to his normal hugeness and they hurried inside.

The witches stopped talking at once. They all stared. They all gasped! Then they all started laughing.

Cackling Carol was furious. 'What's up with you. Haven't you seen a dog before?' The witches were laughing too much to answer. Big Roddy's ears and tail drooped. He knew they were laughing at him. That made Cackling Carol even angrier.

'You rotten lot!' she screeched. 'How dare you be so nasty? Big Roddy will be a jolly sight more useful in guarding against Wizard Egbert than all your silly cats put together!'

The mention of Wizard Egbert brought the witches to order at once. Their amused smirks showed that they didn't believe what Cackling Carol said, but there were more important things to discuss.

Big Roddy trotted off to join all the cats in another part of the cavern. They were keeping an eye on the brooms and spell books. Big Roddy was too upset to even think about chasing the cats. Several of them arched their backs and hissed at him in alarm. Some of them sniggered. But they soon realised that he wasn't going to hurt them and so they ignored him. They went back to washing and grooming themselves. Big Roddy curled up in a dark corner.

The Witch's Dog

6 The Blue Wizard

Meanwhile, the witches were anxiously discussing what to do. All except Cackling Carol. She was still seething and refused to join in. Unfortunately she was so busy sulking, and the other witches were so busy worrying, that no one noticed the big rat sneak into the cavern. It scuttled along the wall towards the cats and brooms. It was a very peculiar rat. It was blue. Blue was Wizard Egbert's favourite colour. Yes, it was Wizard Egbert in disguise.

The ratty Wizard (or Wizardy rat, if you prefer) smiled happily. He could see the piles of spell books behind the cats and brooms. They were what he was after. He had just invented a dangerous and ghastly

spell – his best yet. It turned books of spells into floppy disks! The witches would be without spells for years and years and years! Witches were not very good with new technology. Wizard Egbert knew very well it would take them a very, very long time to learn how to use a computer and download the spells off the disks. And they would have to get electricity supplied to their caverns first before they could even start to use a computer! How would they manage that? It was a truly brilliant spell!

Stealthily, Egbert approached the books. Before he got to work on them, though, he had to do something about the cats. Very quietly he started to recite a cat-sleeping spell. One by one the cats yawned, stretched and fell fast asleep.

But not Big Roddy. The spell didn't affect dogs. Big Roddy heard a very faint whispering and then saw the cats, wide awake one minute, suddenly fall fast asleep the next. Something strange was going on. He cautiously raised his head and looked around. Nothing! But the prickling in his hackles told him something was there.

He glanced at the brooms. They were all exhausted from flying (especially his broom) and they were asleep too. Big Roddy was the only one awake.

Just then a huge blue rat scuttled into sight. It seemed to be looking straight at

Big Roddy but, because he was in such a gloomy corner, the rat couldn't see him, even though he was so big. Big Roddy tensed, ready to spring. He saw the rat creep forwards towards the books. Its long blue whiskers brushed against one of them. It raised a paw and opened its mouth – and that's when Big Roddy leapt. With a mighty 'woof' he shot through the air and slapped two huge paws on the rat's head. It screeched. Big Roddy barked.

The witches came running.

'What has your dog done to our cats?' shrilled one witch when she saw the cats all stretched out on the floor.

'Look, he's eating one of them now!' She grabbed the nearest broom and was just about to wallop Big Roddy with it when another witch noticed the blue rat wriggling under Big Roddy's paws.

'Look! Look! It's Egbert, the blue wizard. The dog has caught the wizard. Bite him, boy. Worry him!'

At once all the witches started shouting the same thing. Big Roddy obligingly sank his teeth into Egbert's bottom and shook him energetically. Egbert wailed. Even though he was a cunning and powerful wizard, Big Roddy's attack had frightened him so much he couldn't remember a single spell. He was helpless. And the witches were loving it!

7 Big Roddy the Hero

Big Roddy gave Egbert another good shaking, which made Cackling Carol and the other witches cackle with glee. Then Witch Matilda came over with a heavy earthenware jar.

'Drop the rat in here, clever dog,' she said. Big Roddy looked at Cackling Carol for her permission. Cackling Carol almost burst with pride. She nodded. Big Roddy dropped the dazed rat into the jar and Witch Matilda slammed the lid on.

'Now, girls, altogether,' she called to her coven. 'Let's say the *Seal-a-jar-for-a-thousand-years* spell.'

At once a weird, howling chant went up. The witches joined hands and swayed from side to side as they cast their spell.

The Witch's Dog

It was a very powerful spell and it took a lot of effort to make. At last there was a sort of a crunching noise and the heavy lid turned and turned and finally stopped. The witches stopped chanting and sighed. It was done. Egbert would be out of the way for a thousand years. What a relief!

The witches crowded round Big Roddy and stroked him and patted him and told him how clever he was. Then they went and crowded round Cackling Carol and told her how clever she was to have found such a clever dog.

'Three cheers for Cackling Carol and Big Roddy!' someone shouted and three cackling cheers went up. The noise woke up the cats and brooms and there was quite a commotion for a while. Witch Matilda dished up pondweed soup and beetle cookies to celebrate. What a night!

It was very, very late when Cackling Carol, Big Roddy and Broom got back home. Cackling Carol was still glowing with pride. Big Roddy had more or less forgotten about what had happened. But he knew his mistress was pleased with him and that was all that mattered.

Cackling Carol gave him a double helping of food and an enormous bone. Broom gently tickled his ears with a few of his bristles. Big Roddy sighed a big contented sigh.

It was great being a witch's dog!

THE END

40

Watch out for other books from

Stephanie Dagg

a, b, c, d, e, f, g, h

U O A K L

E O

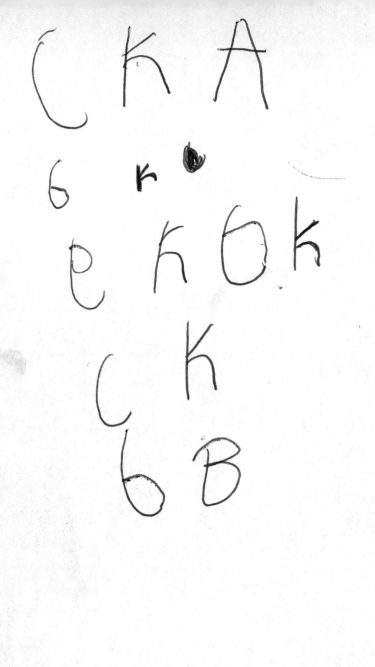